Tomie dePaola

Strega Nona's Gift

Nancy Paulsen Books ☙ An Imprint of Penguin Group (USA) Inc.

For Zoe, Gina, Jarrett
and of course Ralph.

NANCY PAULSEN BOOKS · A division of Penguin Young Readers Group.
Published by The Penguin Group.
Penguin Group (USA) Inc., 375 Hudson Street, New York, NY 10014, U.S.A.
Penguin Group (Canada), 90 Eglinton Avenue East, Suite 700, Toronto, Ontario M4P 2Y3, Canada
(a division of Pearson Penguin Canada Inc.).
Penguin Books Ltd, 80 Strand, London WC2R 0RL, England.
Penguin Ireland, 25 St. Stephen's Green, Dublin 2, Ireland (a division of Penguin Books Ltd.).
Penguin Group (Australia), 250 Camberwell Road, Camberwell, Victoria 3124, Australia
(a division of Pearson Australia Group Pty Ltd).
Penguin Books India Pvt Ltd, 11 Community Centre, Panchsheel Park, New Delhi - 110 017, India.
Penguin Group (NZ), 67 Apollo Drive, Rosedale, Auckland 0632, New Zealand
(a division of Pearson New Zealand Ltd).
Penguin Books (South Africa) (Pty) Ltd, 24 Sturdee Avenue, Rosebank, Johannesburg 2196, South Africa.
Penguin Books Ltd, Registered Offices: 80 Strand, London WC2R 0RL, England.

Design by Marikka Tamura.
Text set in Adobe Jenson.
Calligraphy by Nancy Howell.
The art for this book was created with transparent acrylics on Fabriano 140 lb. handmade watercolor paper.
Library of Congress Cataloging-in-Publication Data is available upon request.
ISBN 978-0-399-25649-3
7 9 10 8 6

Everyone in the little village in Calabria, including Strega Nona, had been busy in their kitchens and at their tables since the month of December began.

First was the Feast of San Nicola – Saint Nicholas – on December 6. The children got to choose the food for this feast because San Nicola was said to love children.

The next feast was on December 13: the Feast of Santa Lucia – Saint Lucy.
In her honor, a special pudding was made with soft wheat berries and
ricotta cheese.

As the weeks went by, Strega Nona kept Big Anthony very busy with errands.

When Bambolona had to go back into the village to help her father,
Papa Bambo, at the bakery, Big Anthony had an idea.

"Strega Nona," Big Anthony said, "since Bambolona isn't here,
I'm ready to help you in the kitchen!"

"Oh," Strega Nona replied, "that is very nice of you, Big Anthony, but I can manage just fine. Besides, you have plenty to do."

"You know," Big Anthony said with a smile, "you're right, Strega Nona."

That was a close one, thought Strega Nona.

December 24 was La Vigilia – Christmas Eve. Every house in
the village was cooking fish for the Feast of the Seven Fishes.
There was no meat served on Christmas Eve, and no meat was
eaten until after the midnight mass.

After the mass, everyone climbed the little hill to Strega Nona's
for her annual Christmas Feast.

There were tables and tables of food.

The Zampognari – shepherds from Abruzzi – were there to sing.
The villagers and the children danced under the stars to celebrate
the birth of baby Jesus.

As a rosy light appeared in the sky, everyone went home for a good, big sleep. After all, there was still a whole week of *festas* left.

On December 31, New Year's Eve, was the Feast of San Silvestro – Saint Sylvester.

"Big Anthony," Strega Nona said, "you must eat your lentils and rice pudding. You won't be prosperous next year if you don't."

"Strega Nona," Big Anthony asked, "will it be all right if I go down to the village to watch the New Year Bonfire? Everyone will be there."

"Of course, *caro*. Only be very careful when the church bell rings at midnight. Hide in a doorway or under an archway. You know that people throw old things they no longer want out the windows. I heard that Signora Anita threw her old stove last year. It nearly killed Signore Mayor."

"I'll be careful," Big Anthony promised.

"Oh, and don't forget to wear your RED underwear. Everyone has to wear their red underwear for *capodanno* – New Year. It brings good luck."

On January 5, the eve of Epifania – Epiphany, the Feast of the Three Kings – once again everyone was cooking. But this time for their animals.

There was a legend that at midnight on the Eve of Epiphany all the animals could speak to each other. It was because the ox and the donkey kept the baby Jesus warm with their breath in the manger.

So, the villagers wanted to give their animals a feast. No one wanted their animals gossiping with each other about how poorly fed or mistreated they were.

Strega Nona was cooking wonderful dishes for her rabbit, her peacock, her dove and especially her goat.

Delicious smells that came out of the kitchen nearly drove Big Anthony crazy. So, when Strega Nona called him in for supper, he almost knocked the door down.

But there at his place at the table was a plain dish of pasta
from Strega Nona's pasta pot. On the counter were four dishes
that looked and smelled so, so good.

"What are those dishes?" Big Anthony asked.

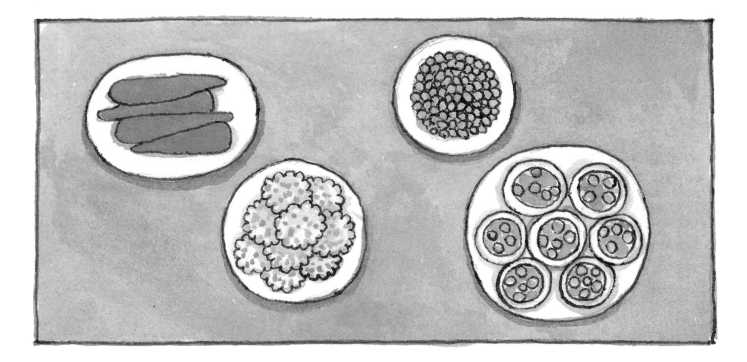

"Those are special dishes for the animals. It's a special night for them. There are carrots for the rabbit, corn cakes for the peacock, sweet seeds for the dove, and turnips stuffed with greens and *ceci* for the goat. As soon as you finish your pasta, take Signora Goat's dish out to her, please."

Big Anthony stopped outside the goat shed. "I'll just take a tiny taste."

"Oh, that's so good," said Big Anthony as he tasted more and more.

"*Santo cielo* – it's all gone!" cried Big Anthony as he looked down at the empty plate.

He quickly filled the plate with hay and oats and left it at the window of the goat shed and quietly ran away.

As Strega Nona tidied up her kitchen, she thought of all the villagers and how they had all worked so hard for their animals all day. And how they probably all had simple suppers like she and Big Anthony.

"I will give everyone a gift," she said as she opened her ancient book.

"I will give everyone a wonderful dream. A dream about food!"

And sure enough, as each one of the villagers drifted off to sleep, everything seemed to turn to food. The fountain poured out milk and honey. The walls turned into ricotta and mozzarella. Bedposts became sausages and the bedsheets changed into sheets of lasagna.

While the villagers were sleeping, the animals gathered in the square
to tell each other what amazing food they had been given that night.

"The sisters gave us the most delicious fried fish," said the cats from
the convent. "What did Strega Nona give you, Signora Goat?"

"I don't know. Big Anthony ate it all before I even had a look at it."

"That's terrible," said the Mayor's dog. "What did you do?"

"I ate his blanket," Signora Goat answered. "I'll bet he's so cold that he doesn't sleep all night."

And Big Anthony didn't sleep. And because he didn't sleep,
he didn't dream about all the wonderful food.
He was not only cold. He was very hungry!

"Here you are, King Anthony," Strega Nona said. "And *buonanotte*."

"*Grazie*, Strega Nona," said Big Anthony. "Thank you."

Then Big Anthony wrapped himself in his new blanket
and knocked on Signora Goat's window.

The next morning, the Day of Epiphany, everyone except Big Anthony
had full stomachs from the dream they received from Strega Nona.

In the early afternoon everyone gathered once again at
Strega Nona's house to celebrate the Feast of Epiphany.

First, everyone took a piece of cake. Whoever had the piece that had a fava bean in it became the king or the queen of the Feast.

"Hurray, look!" some of the men shouted. "It's Big Anthony!"

They carried King Anthony around the table on their shoulders and sat him down in the special chair.

"Well, Big Anthony, because you are king and the Three Kings brought gifts to the child Jesus, what would you like for a gift?" Strega Nona asked.

"A new blanket," Big Anthony answered. "And," he added, "some of that delicious turnip dish you made for Signora Goat last night!"

"Pronto," said Strega Nona.

"Well, Big Anthony, because you are king and the Three Kings brought gifts to the child Jesus, what would you like for a gift?" Strega Nona asked.

"A new blanket," Big Anthony answered. "And," he added, "some of that delicious turnip dish you made for Signora Goat last night!"

"Pronto," said Strega Nona.

He held out the dish of turnips. "Let's have a truce," he said.

And *presto*. The holiday season was over for another year.